The Dog Food Caper

The Dog Food Caper

by Joan M. Lexau
pictures by Marylin Hafner

DIAL BOOKS FOR YOUNG READERS

NEW YORK

Published by
Dial Books for Young Readers
2 Park Avenue
New York, New York 10016

Text copyright © 1985 by Joan M. Lexau
Pictures copyright © 1985 by Marylin Hafner
All rights reserved.
Printed in Hong Kong by South China Printing Co.

The Dial Easy-to-Read logo is a trademark of
Dial Books for Young Readers
A division of New American Library ® TM 1, 162,718

Library of Congress Cataloging in Publication Data
Lexau, Joan M. The dog food caper.
Summary: When his neighbor finds dog food in strange
places all over his house, Willy Nilly asks Miss Happ,
a self-styled witch, to help solve the mystery.
[1. Mystery and detective stories.]
I. Hafner, Marylin, ill. II. Title.
PZ7.L5895Do 1984   [E]   84-1904

W
First Hardcover Printing 1985
ISBN 0-8037-0107-1 (tr.)
ISBN 0-8037-0108-X (lib. bdg.)
2 4 6 8 10 9 7 5 3 1

First Trade Paperback Printing 1987
ISBN 0-8037-0214-0 (ppr.)
2 4 6 8 10 9 7 5 3 1

The art for each picture was created using watercolor, pencil,
and colored inks. It was then color-separated
and reproduced in full color.

Reading Level 2.1

To Rosemary Klein Martin
J. M. L.

To Olivia Brown
M. H.

"But I didn't do it!"

Willy Nilly said.

"I didn't put dog food all over."

Mr. Spring said, "You came here

to take care of Mutt last weekend

like you always do."

"But—" said Willy.

"You and the dog and I

are the only ones who have been here,"

Mr. Spring said.

"All week long I found dog food.

There was some in my good shoes.

I found some under the bed covers.

I got on the bus and put my hand

in my pocket and gave the bus driver

some dog food."

"But I didn't—" Willy said.

Mr. Spring said, "I'm sure

it seemed like a funny thing to do.

But don't do it again

or you can't take care of Mutt.

Good-bye now.

I'll see you Monday."

Mr. Spring left for the weekend.

Willy took Mutt for a walk.

Then he filled up the dog's big bowl.

"See you in the morning,"

he told Mutt.

Willy went next door to his house.

On Saturday morning he went back.

The dog's bowl was empty.

"Good dog, Mutt.

You ate it all up," Willy said.

He took the dog for a run.

When they got back,

Mutt ran to his bowl.

"Hungry again?" Willy said.

He filled the bowl

with Munchie Crunchies.

The dog ate it up quickly.

"You sure were hungry," Willy said.

"Now I'll see what

Mr. Spring left for me."

He found some apple pie in a box.

A note on the box said,

"Willy, ice cream is in the freezer."

Willy opened a drawer to get a spoon.

But he found that the drawer
was full of Munchie Crunchies.
"Oh, no!" Willy said. "Not again!"

He stood on a chair to get a dish.

He found more dog food on a shelf.

"How did this get here?"

Willy thought.

"Maybe it was here all week.

No, Mr. Spring would have found it.

Now he'll think I did this too."

Willy Nilly needed help.

There was only one thing to do.

Willy and Mutt went down the street.

The sign was still

in the store window.

Willy told Mutt,

"There is no Green Street.

Miss Happ lives on Orange Street."

They went down Orange Street
until they came to an old house
with a broom in the driveway.
Next to the broom
was a big orange cat
with big green eyes.
The cat looked at Willy
and said, "HISS!"
The cat looked at Mutt
and took off after him.
Round and round the house
the cat chased the dog.

The front door opened

and Miss Happ looked out.

"Drat, you let that poor dog be!"

she yelled.

The cat ran to the witch

and jumped onto her shoulder.

Miss Happ looked at Willy.

"Oh, it's you," she said.

"Go away and take your dog with you."

Willy said, "I have a problem."

"Too bad," said the witch.

She shut the door.

"You helped me before, Miss Happ,"

Willy yelled.

The witch opened the door.

"Don't just stand there.

Come in," she said.

Willy tied Mutt outside.

He and Miss Happ

went into her house.

"I take care of the dog on weekends,"
Willy said. "But after last weekend
Mr. Spring found dog food
all over his house.

He thinks I put it there.

And now it's there again.

If I don't find out who did it,

I can't take care of Mutt anymore."

"Well, good luck!" said Miss Happ.

"I mean, I want you to help me,"

Willy told her.

"Oh, very well," Miss Happ said.
"I'll start with this magic mix."
She looked in a book and said,
"I'll need some well water."
Willy said, "Do you have a well?
We don't."

Miss Happ went to the sink.

She said, "Does this water

look sick to you?"

Willy said, "No, but—"

"Then it's well water," she said.

"Now I add a pinch of this

and a pinch of that."

She mixed it all up in a bowl.

"Now you go home and give

this magic brew to the dog," she said.

"But how will that tell us

why there is dog food all over?"

Willy asked.

"Beats me," said the witch.

She put the bowl on the floor.

"Din-dins!" she called.

The cat ran to the bowl

and lapped up all the magic brew.

Drat's hair stood on end.

She ran from room to room

and knocked over a lamp

and jumped over the piano.

Then she threw up
and curled up in a corner
and went to sleep.

"I must remember how to make that," said the witch.

"Now we will go to that dog's house and see about your problem."

"Well, I don't know," Willy said.

"Mr. Spring told me not to bring my friends over to play in his house."

The witch looked at him
eyeball-to-eyeball.

"I am a witch.

I work magic.

I DO NOT PLAY!" she yelled.

"Oh," said Willy Nilly.

"Sorry, Miss Happ!"

He took Miss Happ to Mutt's house.

The witch found more dog food
in Mr. Spring's fishing boots
and in back of some books.

They looked at the big bag
of dog food under the sink.
It was full of holes.
"Yes, yes, yes," said Miss Happ.
"That is just like them."
"Like who?" asked Willy.
"Never you mind," the witch said.
"They don't come out in the daytime
so I can't do any more right now.
I'll see you in the morning."
"But how do you know?" Willy asked.
"I have my ways," Miss Happ said.
She left.

Willy took Mutt home with him
and played with him all day.
When it got dark,
he took Mutt next door.
"Sorry, Mutt," Willy said.
"You have to stay home at night.
You are a watchdog."

The next morning Willy went back

to Mutt's house.

Miss Happ was in a chair fast asleep.

She woke up.

"I'm going to watch all night.

That's when they come out,"

she told Willy.

"But it's morning now," Willy said.

The witch looked out the window.

"Who said it wasn't?" she said.

"How did you get in, when
I have the key?" Willy asked.

"I have magic ways,"
Miss Happ said.

Willy looked at the dog's bowl.

It was empty.

White powder was all around it.

"I put that magic powder there,"
Miss Happ told Willy.

"But on the bag it says *flour*,"
Willy said.

The witch said, "Well, I have to keep my magic powder in something."

She walked over to the dog's bowl.

"The magic powder will show

the footprints of whatever

is taking the dog food."

She turned around and yelled, "AHA!

What did I tell you?

Here are some big footprints."

Willy said, "But I think

those are your footprints."

"I was just about to say that.

Why do you say things

I'm just about to say?"

said Miss Happ.

Willy said, "But how can I know

what you are going to say?"

"Ask me!" said the witch.

Willy looked again

at the magic powder.

"Look at these," he said.

"What are they?

They are too small

to be the dog's footprints."

The witch got down and looked.

"I knew it! I knew it!" she said.

"At last I will catch one.

I have been waiting for this day!"

"To catch what?" Willy asked.

"Those are tiny little footprints,"
the witch told him.
"They could only be made by—
an ELF!"

"Wow! An elf!" said Willy.
Miss Happ said, "I must run home
and get the elf cage."
Soon she was back.

She said, "I've had this elf cage
for a long time.
I'll put dog food in it.
Tonight when the elf goes inside,
the door will fall shut.
The elf won't be able to get out."
Willy said, "I can tell Mr. Spring
that the elf hid the dog food."

Miss Happ and Drat went home.

Willy gave Mutt

some Munchie Crunchies.

He played with the dog all day.

When it got dark, Willy left the dog

at Mr. Spring's house and went home.

Before he went to bed,

Willy told his mother and father,

"Tomorrow I will see an elf."

"Sure you will," said his father.

"That's nice, dear," said his mother.

Willy didn't get much sleep.

He looked out the window

again and again.

It was dark at Mutt's house.

In the morning he ran next door.
His mother called after him,
"Take care of the dog quickly.
Don't be late for school."

The witch was asleep again.

She woke up and saw Willy.

"AHA! An elf!" she yelled.

Then she added, "No, no.

You are much too big."

There was a noise from the cage.

"My elf!" said the witch.

"Stand back, Willy!"

She ran to the cage and looked in.

"Oh, no!" she said. "No, no, no!

A silly little mouse got in the cage

and the door fell shut.

The elf got away!

And I waited so long for this day."

There was a noise from the next room.

"Mr. Spring is home," Willy said.

He looked around.

The witch was gone.

Mr. Spring walked in.

"What's that cage doing here?"
he asked Willy.

"Well, see, we tried to catch
the—thing that's taking the dog food,"
Willy told him.

"But a mouse got in the cage."

"A mouse!" said Mr. Spring.
"I see. Come to think of it,
mice do come inside in the fall
when it gets cold out.

And they take food and store it
all over for the winter."

"They do?" asked Willy.

Mr. Spring said,

"I'm sorry I said you were doing it.

I'm glad you found out

it was mice, Willy."

"Well, a witch found out for me,"
Willy told him.

Mr. Spring laughed.

"A witch!

Sure she did, Willy.

You better run to school now.

Will you take care of Mutt

next weekend?"

"Sure," Willy said.

He went outside.

The witch was waiting for him.

"I hope you didn't tell him
about the elf, Willy," she said.

"No, I didn't," Willy said.

"Mr. Spring said that mice—"

Miss Happ said,

"Never mind about mice.

If he knew about the elf,

he would try to catch it.

And that's my elf, Willy."

"Yes. Well, thanks for helping me,"
Willy said.

"Any time," said the witch.

"HISS!" said Drat.